# BUTTERFLIES
# AND MOTHS

First published in Great Britain 1984 by
Webb and Bower (Publishers) Limited
9 Colleton Crescent, Exeter, Devón EX2 4BY

Edited, designed and illustrated by
the E.T. Archive Limited
Chelsea Wharf, 15 Lots Road, London SW10 0QH

Designed by Julian Holland
Picture Research by Anne-Marie Ehrlich
Special photography by Eileen Tweedy
Copyright © text and illustrations E.T. Archive Ltd 1984

**British Library Cataloguing in Publication Data**

Lousada, Sebastian
    Butterflies & moths.—(A Webb & Bower miniature)
    1. Butterflies—Pictorial works
    2. Moths—Pictorial works
    I. Title
    595.78'022'2    QL543

    ISBN 0–86350–014–5

All rights reserved. No part of this publication
may be reproduced, stored in a retrieval system or
transmitted in any form or by any means, electronic,
mechanical, photocopying, recording or otherwise,
without the prior permission of the Copyright holders.

Phototypeset by Text Filmsetters Limited, Orpington, Kent
Printed and bound in Hong Kong by Mandarin Offset International Limited

# BUTTERFLIES AND MOTHS

Sebastian Lousada

*Webb & Bower*
EXETER, ENGLAND

# Swallowtail

Family Papilionidae

*Papilio machaon*

The only Swallowtail to grace our land, this is the largest English butterfly and has a wingspan of up to 9cm. It is more abundant in Europe, Asia and Africa than in England. Although it was common even near London in 1827, it is now restricted to the Norfolk Broads. 'As those parts are fast being drained it is to be feared that we may in time lose this most conspicuous ornament', said the Revd Morris in 1895.

The adults emerge in May, the larger females appearing slightly later. They have a vigorous flapping flight but can also soar and glide for short distances. During courtship the pairs fly together with wide sweeps that decrease to narrower circles as altitude is gained. In hot weather the males sometimes fly long distances, presumably searching for mates.

The spherical yellow eggs are laid singly on milk parsley, fennel or caraway, sticking to the leaf surface with a natural gum. On hatching, the day-feeding caterpillar looks like a small bird-dropping, being black with a white saddle mark. On the third skin-casting it turns black, dotted with orange and alternating with a greenish-white colour. If disturbed, the caterpillar emits a pungent protective odour, somewhat like rotting pineapple, from a forked orange tubercule behind its head. When fully grown, it forms a chrysalis in a reed bed, attaching its hind quarters to a silk pad and spinning a silk girdle around its middle before finally moulting its larval skin.

# Large Meadow Brown

Family Satyridae                                    *Maniola jurtina*

The Meadow Brown or Large Meadow Brown is possibly the most common species of butterfly in England and in 1826 an extraordinary number were seen. The species was first mentioned in 1666 by Christopher Merret. They live throughout Europe and North Africa, flying mainly in hayfields and open places. They have been caught seven miles out at sea but are essentially non-migratory and many never leave the fields where their parents fluttered the year before.

They fly over grass tops from mid-June to late September even on dull days, settling with closed wings quite fearlessly. The males have small spots on the forewings while the females, who carry the males while pairing, have tan patches and eye-like spots.

The eggs are laid on any grasses, and after hatching, the caterpillars eat their eggshells before touching green food. They have forked tails, variable markings and are well camouflaged. They feed only by night, whereas butterfly larvae such as the Swallowtail, eat only by day. When fully grown, they spin a silk pad and hang head downwards to pupate. The 5cm wingspan adults hatch a month later. There are two overlapping broods of young a year.

# Silver-Washed Fritillary

Family Nymphalidae

*Argynnis paphia*

This insect was named by Moses Harris in 1775. The hind-wings look like a green beach washed by a silver sea but previously it had the name 'Greater silver-streaked Fritillary'. In Europe where it occurs up to 1500m, it is known as the 'Emperor's cloak'. There is also a similar species in North America.

These large fritillaries are lovers of tall trees, never being found far from woodlands where they fly powerfully over bracken and soar above the tree tops. At night they sleep in the foliage. The females lay their eggs in the crevices of oak bark. Two weeks later they hatch and the tiny caterpillars usually hibernate from August until the end of March. With the warmer weather, they awake and crawl or are blown down the trunks in search of sweet violet plants. Once they start feeding, they grow fast and develop large spines for camouflage and protection, a pair of which project over the head like horns.

They pupate hanging head downwards, forming a silver-studded chrysalis which wiggles violently if touched. In July the pupae split and the 7cm-wingspan butterflies emerge. The females are larger than the males and quite commonly take on a dark silvery-grey form known as 'Aberration Valesina'.

This most English of butterflies lives mainly in southern England and is plentiful in the New Forest. It is only occasionally found north of the Lake District.

Pl. 10.

# Red Admiral

Family Nymphalidae                                    *Vanessa atalanta*

The Red Admiral or 'Alderman' butterfly lives throughout Europe, North Africa, Canada and North America but is not a permanent resident north of the Alps. Also called the 'Admirable' butterfly, its name probably comes from the red bands across the forewings which are scarlet like the uniforms of early admirals. Both sexes are similar. They are commonly seen in gardens, feeding off buddleia or ivy blossoms and they are also partial to fallen apples and sap.

In May, the eggs are laid singly on nettle leaves – the caterpillars especially like eating the seeds of the nettles. The colour of the caterpillar varies, usually being dusky-green with yellowish lines along the back and sides. The solitary larva lives and feeds in a folded leaf lined with silk which protects it from most predators. When fully grown, the larvae tie together several leaves and pupate inside, head downwards; their gold-pointed pupae hatch after two weeks.

If Red Admirals did not migrate, they would not be seen in England, for although they do breed there, they are unfortunately unable to survive the alternate damp and frosts of the winter. With a wingspan of up to 7cm they are strong fliers, even by night; some try to return south in the autumn. Young adults arrive from May to September, breeding as long as there is warm weather.

# Painted Lady

Family Nymphalidae                                    *Vanessa cardui*

The Painted Lady or 'Good King Henry' is one of the most widespread butterfly species in the world. It migrates to England in varying numbers each season from North Africa, occasionally flying in large swarms. Thomas Mouffet wrote in 1658 that in 1553, 'An infinite army of butterflies flew... and did infect the grasse, herbs, houses and garments of men with bloudy drops as though it had rained bloud'.

In 1828, a huge swarm flew over part of Switzerland and took several hours to pass. In Europe, large swarms of Painted Ladies are thought to be forerunners of a good quail season. This butterfly becomes so numerous in North Africa that it is literally forced to migrate in order to survive.

The newly arrived migrants head straight for the hills. After an elaborate June courtship the females descend to the valleys where they lay their eggs singly on thistles, burdock, and artichokes. The young caterpillar spins a layer of silk and lives between it and the underside of the leaf. As it grows larger it moves to the upper surfaces of the leaves but still spins a silk roof above itself, eating entire leaves except the largest veins. The brown caterpillar is rather stout for its length and pupates hanging upside-down. The chrysalis is sandy-grey and hatches in August or September.

Like the Red Admiral, the Painted Lady does not reside year-round in England. Some attempt to hibernate with the colder weather but do not usually survive.

# Small Tortoiseshell

Family Nymphalidae                                  *Aglais urticae*

> It is wonderful, beautiful, the wings are light bloud
> colour, dipt with black spots, they shine with smal
> long beams dispersedly drawn like threads to the
> very outermost of the coat and this is adorned
> within with golden crooked lines like the moon...
>
> *Thomas Mouffet, 1658*

The Small Tortoiseshell is one of the most common and
long-living butterflies and is found in Europe, Asia and
Japan at altitudes of up to 2500m. It can see some colours
and is more strongly attracted to purple than pink. Pairing
occurs in the spring with the male pursuing the female on
foot, tapping her with his antennae and chasing her every-
where.

Fifty to one hundred eggs are laid on the undersides of
stinging nettle leaves. On hatching, they spin a communal
silk web which is used as a roof at night and a platform for
sunbathing during the resting periods between feeding.
When there is a food shortage the entire brood moves on
and makes another web. The caterpillars are covered in
spines and are protected as a large group because of the
difficulty a predator has in singling out any one individual.
When fully grown, they split up and hang upside-down in
the undergrowth to pupate.

Two weeks later in July they emerge. A second brood
hatches in late August and the adults hibernate often in
hollow trunks, until spring.

# Peacock

Family Nymphalidae                                         *Inachis io*

The Peacock was said by Thomas Mouffet in 1658 to be 'the queen or chief of all, for in the outermost part of the wings . . . four adamants glistering in a beazil of hyacinth do shew wonderful rich . . . and shine curiously like stars'.

The 'Peacock's eye by day' as it is also called, lays its eggs in untidy batches on stinging nettles. They show the same web behaviour as Small Tortoishells, but when almost fully grown, they split up into groups of two or three to share a leaf on which to rest while not feeding. They are spiny and black with white spots, and have red hind legs. They range further than many other caterpillars just before pupating and often climb up tree trunks.

The pupae have a metallic sheen and the adults emerge after two weeks with a 6cm wingspan. The Peacock is common throughout Europe except in the far north and the two sexes are similar in size and colouring. They hibernate through the winter in corners of buildings, rabbit holes and evergreens. If disturbed, they rub their wings together making a hissing sound not unlike that of a snake. On awakening in spring, they flutter along in parks, gardens and open woods, their wings making a characteristic sound like silk on silk.

During courtship the female sits on the bare earth with open wings while the male flies high in the air. Their undersides are well camouflaged and adults may live up to ten months including their winter sleep.

# Camberwell Beauty

Family Nymphalidae                                    *Nymphalis antiopa*

> This is one of the scarcest flies of any known in England nor do
> we know of above three or four that were ever found here . . .
>
> *Moses Harris, 1766*

On a number of occasions, this great prize of British lepi-
dopterists was caught near the village of Camberwell (now
engulfed by London). It has never bred in England, but in
the United States and Europe the 'Mourning Cloak' is common. It is also known as the 'Grand Surprise', 'Willow
Beauty', or 'White Petticoat' and has always had an erratic
presence in England, being a late summer migrant.

Eggs are laid on willow, sallow or birch leaves. The
gregarious caterpillars make a web to live in and when fully
grown they hang upside-down to pupate. After three weeks
they emerge and live for up to ten months, hibernating
through the winter. In spring they are often the first butterflies on the wing, flying strongly and gliding over tree tops.
They never feed on flowers, preferring sap and fruit.

It is possible that some fly to our shores, but many are
stowaways, hibernating among pit props stacked for export
from Scandinavia and getting free rides to English ports.

Fresh specimens have yellow borders which fade to
white with age. For many years it was thought that English
specimens always had white borders. An old specimen in
the British Museum was found to have had its borders
painted white by a dishonest dealer who covered the yellow
in order to sell it as a native.

# Comma

Family Nymphalidae                                  *Polygonia c-album*

The Comma is supremely camouflaged and hibernates on tree trunks looking very like a dead leaf. Its name comes from the curious pale marks on the undersides of its hind-wings. The comma's flight is rapid and jerky and it visits gardens but prefers to live among trees. Newly awoken Commas find each other by means of special scales on their wings which emit odours attractive to each other over large distances.

Eggs are laid singly, usually on the tops of nettles. Immediately after hatching, the larvae crawl under the leaves and start eating. When fully grown they have spikes and a white splash which makes them resemble a bird-dropping. They pupate head downwards and form an odd-shaped chrysalis which hatches in two weeks. In England there are two broods – the first on the wing in early July, and the second in late August which hibernates through the winter. In Europe they have a wide range up to an altitude of 1800m. In North America, 'Angle-Wings' (a similar species) are common.

The population of this butterfly has fluctuated vastly, possibly because of the effects of bad spring weather. Until 1850, they were plentiful, but by 1900, they were confined to the Wye valley. Since then, they have spread once more and can often be seen opening and shutting their wings before flying in search of flowers, sap or rotting fruit.

# Purple Emperor

Family Nymphalidae                                    *Apatura iris*

Only the male of this rare butterfly has a purple sheen on its wings. Also known as the 'Emperor of Morocco', it is found in extensive woodlands and in Europe is called the 'Large Lustre Butterfly'.

Purple Emperors have powerful flight and the male usually stays at tree-top level, flying through his territory in the early morning but returning to a tree before noon.

Perched on the outermost spray of some commanding
oak . . . he sits, generally with his attention directed
outwards as an island's king should be, conscious that at
home he is secure.                          *The Revd Morris, 1895*

The adults feed on sap, honeydew, rotting carcasses and cow manure. They may also be seen drinking from puddles. They fly in mid-July and live for one month.

The females often fly low, looking for sallow on which to lay their eggs. The conspicuous eggs are laid singly. The grey caterpillar first eats its eggshell and after the first moult, horns appear on its head. When still quite small it hibernates and in spring awakens and turns green with chlorophyll from the leaves. If disturbed it moves its head vigorously from side to side. The horned chrysalis is formed on a leaf stalk and resembles a folded sallow leaf.

Avid collectors designed a net on a fifty-foot pole to catch the elusive males and others used rotting meat to lure them down within easier reach.

# Large Blue

Family Lycaenidae                                    *Maculinea arion*

Until 1924, little was known of the curious life of the Large Blue butterfly. Unfortunately, although still found very locally in Europe, it is now extinct in England.

The greenish-blue eggs are laid singly on wild thyme buds in June. The females invariably pick plants growing on top of ants' nests and the egg takes ten days to hatch. The small cannibalistic caterpillar looks like and feeds on blossoms. After its third moult it stops feeding and starts to wander until it meets a red ant. The ant recognizes it and starts to milk the gland on the caterpillar's back which then exudes sweet liquid. The caterpillar hunches up and the ant promptly carries it down to its nest. It lives there, being milked by the ants and in return feeds on young ant grubs. It turns a pale colour, hibernates for the winter and in spring resumes feeding again until June.

The pupa is suspended on silk in the nest. Three weeks later it hatches and the butterfly crawls along the tunnels to a grass stem where it can expand and dry its wings. The wingspan is up to 4cm and the adult has a flight strong enough to handle the coastal winds of its haunts.

The Large Blue has always been rare but when its secret habitats became known, collectors went to Cornwall and dug up ants' nests to get the pupae. Even so, until very recently there were thinly scattered colonies throughout southern England.

# Large Copper

Family Lycaenidae                                           *Lycaena dispar*

> I cannot but with some regret recall . . . when almost any
> number of this dazzling fly was easily procurable . . . for
> our cabinets.                                    *The Revd Morris, 1895*

The English Large Copper had become extinct forty-seven
years before Morris's lament. The species was only disco-
vered in 1795 and was rare by 1840. Drainage of the fens
was blamed by Morris but over-collecting was probably the
main reason for this insect's decline. Until 1847 specimens
could still be bought for £1 to £20 each.

In 1927 a similar Dutch variety was introduced and
now lives in Wood Walton Fen in Huntingdonshire. In
Europe the subspecies *L.d. dispar* is confined to Friesland in
Holland, but the other one *L.d. rutila* is more widespread.

Females lay single eggs on the great water dock. The
caterpillars first feed only on the leaf cuticle but soon perfo-
rate the leaves. Before hibernating, they turn purplish-
brown to match the fading colours and breathe so slowly
that they can withstand total immersion in the fens.

In spring they turn back to green. The fully grown
caterpillar rarely moves and then only glides sluggishly.
They may be 'farmed' by ants in the same way as the Large
Blues, and this helps reduce the risk of their being parasitized. They pupate attached by a girdle to a silk pad which
they spin on a leaf. The adults have a 4cm wingspan and fly
from late June until the end of July, swift and active in the
reeds.

# Black-veined White

Family Pieridae                                              *Aporia crataegi*

In 1925 the last Black-veined White was seen in England. They still live, however, in Europe up to 2000m, doing considerable damage in some years to orchards. In the 1800s they were very widespread in southern England and Wales but gradually declined in numbers until their mysterious extinction.

The eggs are laid in late summer on thorns and fruit trees. On hatching, colonies of up to twenty spin a silk web in the fork of a tree on which they spend the winter, hibernating from October onwards. They feed only in morning and evening, moving up growing shoots and then walking backwards as they devour them. When young, they are black, but as they grow to their full size of 8cm, they rapidly become hairier. The colonies have a disagreeable smell to help fend off predators, but if still disturbed, they speedily crawl into the leafiest part of the tree and only when danger is past, do they return to their communal lifestyle. When full size, the caterpillars separate and pupate on pads of silk on thick branches. The pupae are quite conspicuous and many may be lost to hungry birds.

The large adult butterflies are on the wing in July, slowly flapping around neglected orchards and lanes. The females have semi-transparent wings and spiral upwards in thermal currents during their courtship.

# Large White

Family Pieridae                                    *Pieris brassicae*

The Large White has a history as a garden pest. Pliny described setting up a mare's skull on a stake in the middle of the cabbage patch to scare them away. Until the last century in southern France, eggshells were placed on poles in the garden so that females, attracted by the colour white, would lay their eggs on them and the young would starve.

The female Large White has been recorded as laying four eggs a minute. They are laid in irregular batches on cabbages, hedge-mustard, turnips, nasturtiums and radishes. The caterpillars are gregarious when young and as they grow they often form lines along the edge of a leaf and devour it as they move backwards. The caterpillars smell unpleasant. Richard South noted in 1906 that 'the unpleasantness of the odour is greatly intensified if the caterpillars are trodden upon'.

When fully grown they become solitary and pupate attached to leaves, stems or fences. Many get parasitized by Ichneumon wasps which lay their eggs inside the caterpillar's body. The young slowly eat their way out as they hatch. Large Whites overwinter in the chrysalis and emerge in May, expanding their wings to more than 7cm. A second brood hatches in August and flies until October. They have an uneven, flapping flight and occasionally migrate to England from the continent.

In 1666 a vast cloud that looked like a snowstorm and darkened the sun was reported.

# Orange Tip

Family Pieridae

*Anthocharis cardamines*

Sixty-eight species of butterfly can be found in England. The Orange Tip or 'Wood Lady' has a weak fluttery flight and likes to follow winding lanes and hedges. Only the males have orange tips to their wings and both sexes can be seen from the end of April until June. Their undersides are a beautiful camouflaged green and the male tucks his forewings down to hide the orange tips while it is resting.

With a wingspan of up to 5cm, the Orange Tip inhabits most of Europe up to 2000m and in the United States, a similar but slightly smaller species called the Falcate Orange Tip, is widespread.

Creamy-white eggs are laid singly in May, on the flower heads of the cuckoo flower, (*Cardamine pratensis*, from which the butterfly's specific name comes), jack-by-the-hedge, charlock and honesty. The eggs turn grey just before hatching and the young caterpillars eat seed pods, resting lengthwise on the pod to remain less noticeable. During these early stages, the larvae exude sweet droplets which are collected by ants. The caterpillars are cannibalistic, attacking and eating other larvae on sight. It is interesting to note that cannibalism and a relationship with ants are often connected.

The fully grown caterpillars pupate by attaching themselves to a stem with silk threads and then spinning a girdle to hold themselves securely. The boat-shaped chrysalides are pointed at both ends and the Orange Tips hibernate in this form before hatching in spring.

# Clouded Yellow

Family Pieridae *Colias crocea*

The Clouded Yellow or Spotted Saffron butterfly is a migrant species which arrives in England from southern Europe during the summer and autumn. The early arrivals may breed and sometimes even have two broods in southern England. In warmer climates, this insect has continual broods and does not hibernate.

In 1941 many thousands of Clouded Yellows reached England and some fields turned yellow because of their numbers. The migrations occur in cycles but there have been far fewer in recent times owing to intensive agriculture. A lighthouse-keeper saw a swarm of these butterflies flying north in the spring and then south as winter was approaching. This suggests they may attempt to flee the colder weather.

The Revd Morris described the Clouded Yellow's habitat as 'the California of the entomological speculator'. They like clover and lucerne fields where the golden females, which have a wingspan of up to 6cm, lay their eggs one at a time on the upper surfaces of leaves. The eggs are yellow but turn grey before hatching. At first, the young green caterpillars eat only the top surface of the leaves but as they grow they strip entire plants. They pupate attached to a stem.

In the United States, Orange Sulphurs are a very common, similar species.

# Brimstone

Family Pieridae

*Gonepteryx rhamni*

The Brimstone may be the butter-coloured fly from which came the word butterfly. It is also known as the 'Lemon-bird' or 'Lemon leaf'. Only the male has yellow colouring, the female is a greeny-white and lays her eggs singly on the underside of buckthorn leaves. If more than one egg is found, it usually means that more than one female has laid there. The caterpillars are solitary and very well camouflaged, looking more like shadows than living things. The pupae are equally well disguised, hanging horizontally under leaves, slung in a silk girdle and resembling curled leaves.

Two weeks later, at the end of July, the adults emerge and zigzag hurriedly in the air on their 7cm wings. They absorb the sun until frost kills all the flowers and they are forced to hibernate. When dormant, both sexes look like leaves and are thus safe as they sleep through the dampest and coldest of conditions among ivy or other bushes. They inhabit Europe wherever their foodplants grow, at altitudes of up to 2000m.

The awakened Brimstone is the first sign of a new spring. The males always awake first, usually in early March, and fly strongly, waiting for females so eagerly that they will dash at pieces of fluttering white paper. The females wake two to three weeks later and the males are attracted to them both by scent and sight. They live until early June.

# Red Underwing

Family Catocalidae                                    *Catocala nupta*

When it goes upon its feet and its wings close to its body,
looketh dun; but when it flieth with the wings strecht
forth the innermost wings are carnation.

*Thomas Mouffet, 1658*

The beautifully ridged eggs of this fine moth species are laid
on the bark of poplar or willow trees. The active whitish-
grey caterpillars feed at night having hairy protuberances
along their sides which help them blend into the branches
upon which they rest during the day. When fully grown in
May or June they pupate forming a strong coarse cocoon
which is spun between leaves.

The moths hatch in August or September and are more
common some years than others. They like to sit on walls
and may often be seen on telephone poles, usually one to a
pole. They are alert, often flying in the daytime, their
irregular flight and red underwings being quite startling to
pursuing predators. Underwings are found throughout
Europe and into the Indo-Asian region.

Moths can be caught using light traps or by sugaring –
an old method of mixing sugar, beer and rum together and
spreading it on tree trunks in various places. Attracted by
the smell, the moths get drunk and are caught easily.

In the seventeenth century, most moths were consi-
dered evil and some people, according to Mouffet, would
'hang a horse tail pulled off upon the door and... wittily
believe that moths are kept away thereby'.

# Emperor Moth

Family Saturniidae                    *Saturnia pavonia*

The Emperor moth or 'Night Peacock' is England's only silk moth and it comes from a family containing the largest moth in the world, the Atlas moth, with a 29cm wingspan. The eyespots on the wings scare predators, but this moth is not related to the Peacock butterfly whose spots serve the same purpose.

The large female Emperors are rather lethargic, flying only rarely and always under the cover of night. The smaller males have tawny hindwings and fly well by day. They have large plumed antennae used for locating females from distances of up to four kilometres and will even be attracted to containers that once held a newly-hatched female.

The eggs are laid in strings and are glued on heather, hawthorn or other plants. The larvae feed in June and July. They are dark when young and small enough to hide, but as they grow larger and more obvious they turn a handsome green with velvet black bands and raised spots of golden yellow. They pupate in August.

All silk moths spin protective cocoons around their pupae. The fine inner layer of these cocoons may be unwound in certain species and used as silk. The Emperor's cocoon is pear-shaped with a one-way spined exit at the narrower end which enables the moths to emerge (in May) but keeps predators out. They live on heaths and moors in much of England and Europe.

# Death's Head Hawk Moth

Family Sphingidae

*Acherontia atropos*

> If night moths go into a bee-hive and trouble bees in the
> night, bury dung mingled with the marrow of an oxe
> and by the smell thereof these unquiet disturbes will
> promptly fall down.
>
> *Thomas Mouffet, 1658*

The Death's Head Hawk moth lives throughout all
Europe and Africa. It is the largest moth to migrate to
England and has a 12cm wingspan. The eerie skull effigy on
its thorax led to its names of 'Wandering Death Bird', and
its scientific name stems from the River Acheron in Hades
and Atropos, one of the Fates. All members of the family
Sphingidae have caterpillars which rest with their heads
raised like sphinxes.

Also called the 'Bee Tyger', it flies in pitch black dark-
ness and has a great liking for honey, entering the hives and
robbing the bees using its short strong proboscis that is
specially adapted for piercing honeycombs. In Italy, 154
were once taken from a hive. If disturbed, the moth can
make a loud squeak, once thought to be used to confuse the
bees into thinking it was their queen.

Death's Heads lay green eggs on potato plants and after
hatching they grow in to 120cm 'Tatur Dogs' as country
people call them. In the autumn they pupate in frail under-
ground cells, flying about a year later.

It was believed in central France that the dust from
their wings would blind you if it fell on your eyes.

# Hummingbird Hawk Moth

Family Sphingidae                    *Macroglossa stellatarum*

The Hummingbird Hawk moth has always been a harbinger of goodwill and joy. Unlike the adult Emperor moth which has no tongue with which to feed the Hummingbird has a very long proboscis to probe jasmine, honeysuckle and other flowers. As it hovers, its wings beat so rapidly that they appear as a haze and the resulting high-pitched hum can be heard by most women but not by men who lose the ability to hear sounds at that pitch in adolescence.

Up to 200 eggs are laid, usually on unopened buds of bedstraw, in July and August. In warm weather, the caterpillars may reach full size in three weeks before pupating in flimsy cocoons which hatch three weeks later. In southern Europe and the rest of the Paleartic there is often more than one brood and the adults may be present all year round. The moth reaches England by migrating north in spring.

They fly by day and one was timed to visit 194 flowers in 7 minutes and seen to return to the same flowers each day at the same time. They are swift fliers and hover in front of any bright objects including brass door-knobs and greenhouse glass in front of orchids. They hibernate in winter but those which survive the English weather rarely find mates the next year.

On D-Day a small swarm of these insects invaded England from France in opposition to the Allies who invaded France from England.

# Peppered Moth

Family Selidosemidae                              *Biston betularia*

The Peppered moth or, 'Pepper and Salt moth', is an interesting example of how species continually evolve and adapt in order to survive.

In the 1840s Peppered moths were common, living in woods and gardens throughout England. By 1906 it was noticed that an extremely dark variety was becoming more frequent in certain areas such as the south-west of Yorkshire, Lancashire, Cheshire, Lincolnshire and some parts of Staffordshire. In 1945 it was realized that although a normal Peppered moth beautifully matches lichens growing on clean trees, only the dark 'carbonaria' forms are adequately camouflaged against birds in the lichenless city grime. The areas where 'carbonaria' was becoming prevalent were all heavy industrial regions. Even in some rural areas, however, 'carbonaria' was common and for some time this was not understood. People suggested that they grew darker as they bred further north, but this idea was quickly dropped. It now seems that the Peppered moth wanders a great deal and even though the 'carbonaria' form is obvious against the pale tree trunks in rural areas, its numbers constantly reinforce those of its rural relatives, out in the country.

The brown caterpillars are exactly like walking twigs and can cling to a branch with a force ninety-two times their own weight. They feed on oak and the 2cm-wingspan adults fly in May and June.

# Sources and Acknowledgements

Eleazar Albin, *Insectorum Angliae*, 1731, p.13

John Curtis, *British Entomology*, 1828, p.39, 43

Edward Donovan, *The Natural History of British Insects*, 1742, p.15, 19, 37.

Moses Harris, *L'Aurélian ou l'Histoire Naturelle des Chenilles, Chrysalides, Phalenes et Papulions Anglois*, 1794, p.11, 29, 35, 45, 47

H.N. Humphreys and J.O. Westwood, *British Butterflies and their Transformations*, 1851, p.9, 25, 27

W.F. Kirby, *European Butterflies and Moths*, 1882, p.23

W. Lewin, *The Insects of Great Britain*, 1795, p.5

John Miller, *Insects and Plants*, 1780, p.21

Benjamin Wilkes, *The English Butterflies and Moths*, 1747-60, p.7, 17, 31, 33

*Title page*: title page from J.C. Sepp, *De Wonderen Gods in de Minst-Geachte Schepseleen*, 1762-95

Most of the photographs were taken by Eileen Tweedy
Many of the illustrations are reproduced by permission of the Council of the Linnean Society of London and the publishers would like to thank the librarian for her help in the production of the book